NOTHING AT ALL

BY WANDA GA'G

SMITHMARK

This edition published in 1998 by SMITHMARK Publishers,
a division of U.S. Media Holdings, Inc.,
115 West 18th Street, New York, NY 10011.

SMITHMARK Books are available for bulk purchase for sales
promotion and premium use. For details write or call the manager of special sales, SMITHMARK Publishers, 115 West 18th Street,
New York, NY 10011.

ISBN: 0-7651-0859-3

Printed in Hong Kong
10 9 8 7 6 5 4 3 2 1

Library of Congress Catalog Card Number: 98-60770

NOTHING AT ALL

ONCE UPON A TIME there were three little orphan dogs. They were brothers. They lived in a far forgotten corner of an old forgotten farm in three forgotten kennels which stood there in a row.

One of the kennels had a pointed roof and in it lived Pointy, the dog with pointed ears.

Another kennel had a curly roof and in it lived Curly, the dog with curly ears.

The middle kennel had a roundish roof and in it lived the third dog, but whether he had round ears nobody knew, for he was a dog whom no one could see. He was invisible.

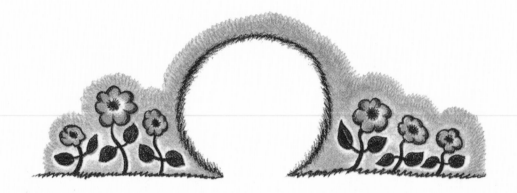

He was not very tall
Nor yet very small;
He looked like nothing,
Like nothing at all.

And that was his name — Nothing-at-all.

Nothing-at-all was happy enough, for although no one could see him, he had just as much fun as any other dog.

He could jump and run and eat. He could hear and see and smell. He could bark and romp and play with his two little puppy brothers.

And Pointy said to Nothing-at-all, "We love you even if we can't see you."

And Curly said, "We know you are a really truly dog even if we can't see you. We can't see the wind either but the wind is real. And we can't see smells but smells are *very* real."

And Nothing-at-all said, "Oh, I suppose it takes all kinds of dogs to make a world, both see-able and unsee-able ones, so why should I worry?"

And he was as happy as any dog could be until there came a day when something happened.

It was a warm and drowsy day. Pointy was lying in his pointed kennel, Curly was lying in his curly kennel, and Nothing-at-all was lying in his roundish kennel. They were dozing, all three, when the sound of voices roused them from their dreams.

"Oh look!" cried a boy-voice. "Here are some dog kennels in this far forgotten corner of the old forgotten farm."

"With dogs in them?" asked a girl-voice.

The boy looked into one kennel and said, "Yes! There's a curly-eared dog in here."

Next he looked into another kennel and said, "And a pointy-eared dog in here!"

Then he looked into the middle kennel, but since only invisible Nothing-at-all was in there, he saw nothing. "The roundish kennel is empty," he said. "Nothing in it at all."

Gently and carefully the girl reached for Pointy; gently and carefully the boy reached for Curly, but the two little dogs were frightened and began to whimper.

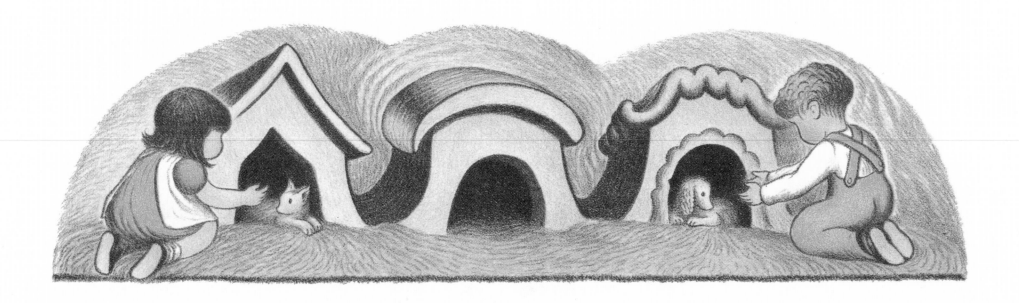

"Don't cry, little pointy-eared dog,"
said the girl. "We won't hurt you. We'll
adopt you both and give you milk to
drink and bones to nibble."

And the boy said, "Don't cry, little
curly-eared dog. We'll be kind to you.
We won't ever hit you or kick you, or
pick you up by your neck or your tail,
or with your legs dangling down."

When Pointy and Curly heard this, they knew they would be safe and happy, so they snuggled into the children's arms and went back to sleep.

And then they were carried away to a new and happy home, while poor little Nothing-at-all was left behind. But do you think he sat down and cried? Oh no — he had a plan!

"I'll just be very quiet and go with them," he thought. "After a while they'll get used to me and find out I'm a really truly dog even though they can't see me. Then they'll adopt me too. And they'll never hurt me but will give me milk to drink. And bones to nibble. I think I will like it very much!"

Those were his thoughts as he trotted after the boy and the girl and his two puppy brothers.

But it was a long long road, and soon his little invisible legs felt so weary and his big invisible eyes felt so blinky that he had to sit down and rest. His eyes blinked once and twice and thrice, and then he was fast asleep. When he awoke he was all alone.

"Oh, where is everybody?" he cried. "I must run and find them!"

He ran to the puddle pond. No one was there.

He ran round the blossom bushes. No one was there.

He ran past the poppy patch. No one was there.

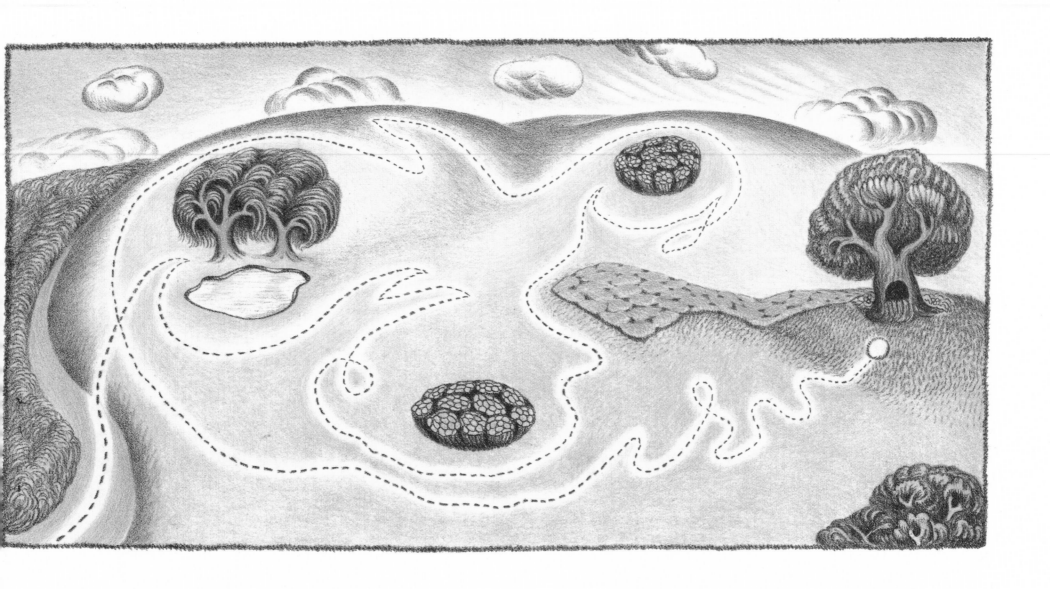

Back and forth he went, in and out, over and under, in twists and curves and zigzags, but no one was anywhere.

At last he found a hollow tree which looked something like a kennel. He crept into it —and, because he felt so lonely and so very much like nothing, he murmured sadly to himself:

"Oh, I'm not very tall
And not very small;
I look like nothing,
Like nothing at all!"

As he finished, a voice said, "I can't see you, but aren't you that empty space in the tree trunk?" It was a bird who spoke.

"Yes," said the little dog. "My name is Nothing-at-all, and that's what I look like too. I never minded it before, but now I long to look like other dogs so the boy and the girl can see me, and so they'll give me milk to drink and bones to nibble, and never pick me up by my neck or my tail, but adopt me for their pet as they did my two puppy brothers."

The bird laughed.

"That's a long speech for an empty space to make!" he said. "But I can understand how you feel, and I might be able to help you."

"But you're only a bird," said Nothing-at-all. "How can you help me?"

"I am a JACKDAW," said the bird proudly, "and as such it is my task to carry home everything I see. Once I even found a Book of Magic — wait! I'll be right back," and the bird was gone.

When he returned, the jackdaw said, "It's just as I thought. In the Book of Magic there is a chapter called NOTHINGNESS AND SOMETHINGNESS. And it says that he who is Nothingy, yet wishes to be Somethingy, must get up at sunrise and whirl around and around and around. While whirling thus, he must say this magic chant:

I'm busy
Getting dizzy.

This, says the book, he must do nine days in a row at sunrise, and he shall see what he shall see. Goodbye, I'm off!" and the bird was gone.

The next morning before sunrise Nothing-at-all was wide awake and ready to try his magic. As soon as the sun peeped over the hilltop, he began whirling and twirling and swirling, and he said:

"I'm busy
Getting dizzy
I'm busy
Getting dizzy."

After he had stopped whirling, what do you suppose had happened?

Do you think he was a dog whom anyone could see? No, he wasn't. He still looked Nothingy but now his Nothingness had a shape! When he held up his paw, he couldn't see the paw but he could see a paw-shaped space, and he was very happy about that.

"Well done!" cried a voice which was the jackdaw's. "You are a pleasant-looking shape, I must say. Keep it up!" and the bird was gone.

The next day Nothing-at-all worked at his magic as before. As soon as the sun peeped over the hilltop, he whirled and twirled and swirled, and said:

"I'm busy
Getting dizzy
I'm busy
Getting dizzy."

When he stopped, the jackdaw came and said, "Yes, the magic is working well. That's a fine black spot you have on your back now. Keep it up!" and the bird was gone.

The third morning at sunrise Nothing-at-all
whirled and twirled and swirled, and said:
"I'm busy
Getting dizzy
I'm busy
Getting dizzy
I'm busy
Getting dizzy."

When he sat down to rest, the jackdaw came
and said, "You're doing better than I expected.
You've added quite a few spots today. Goodbye!"
and the bird was gone.

The fourth day, after Nothing-at-all had whirled and twirled and swirled and repeated his busy-dizzy chant, the jackdaw came and said, "You are certainly working hard at your magic task. That black tail-tip is a beauty, I must say!"

The little dog was so pleased that he wagged his tail wildly, and although the *tail* was still invisible, its black tip showed the wagging plainly enough. The jackdaw laughed at this and then disappeared.

By the fifth day, Nothing-at-all's eyes were visible.

By the sixth day, his nose and mouth could be seen.

On the seventh day his tongue was visible.

On the eighth day his ears and paws could be seen.

And then came the ninth day.

Nothing-at-all whirled and twirled and swirled as he had never done before, and he said:

> "I'm busy
> Getting dizzy
> I'm busy
> Getting dizzy
> I'm busy
> Getting dizzy
> I'm busy
> Getting dizzy,"

until he was so dizzy that the whole world seemed to swirl around with him.

When he stopped to rest, the jackdaw came. "Good work!" he cried. "Now you are SOMETHING after all — a really truly see-able dog! And a most lovable round-eared puppy you are, to be sure. Good luck! Goodbye!" and the jackdaw flew away.

Now the little dog was so happy that he jumped to his feet and barked and picked up sticks and tore about wildly.

Round and round in a circle he ran.
With leaps and bounds and somersaults he ran.
In twists and curves and zigzags he ran.
Back and forth, in and out, over and under,
around blossom bushes and puddle ponds and
poppy patches he ran.

And then he stopped ..... for ——

There in front of him were the boy and the girl.
They were coming from the far forgotten corner of the
old forgotten farm, and were pulling a long red cart
on which were:
>the pointed kennel
>>the curly kennel
>>>and the roundish kennel, all in a row!

With a run and a jump, the round-eared puppy hopped into his roundish kennel, and now he too was taken to a new and happy home. All along the way he wagged his black-tipped tail, and with joyful barks he said:

"I've always been small
And not very tall;
I used to look like nothing at all.
I'm still rather small
And not a bit tall,
But now I'm a see-able dog after all!"

But the boy and the girl didn't know what the little dog was saying. Nor did they know what Pointy and Curly were saying when they met their long-lost brother again.

But maybe,
      perhaps,
            almost surely, they said:
   "How happy we'll be, all three of us here;
with our dear old kennels to live in, and the
two kind children to play with. And oh, little
Something-after-all, it *is* so nice to SEE you!"

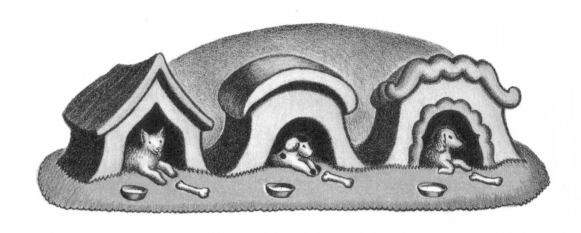

THE END